# LUNCHROOM REVENGE

Eric Hobbs

Illustrated by
DEE Fish

Astoria Press
4026 Highland Springs Drive
Kokomo, IN 46902

Publisher's Note: This is a work of fiction. Names, characters, places, and incidents are a product of the author's imagination. Locales and public names are sometimes used for atmospheric purposes. Any resemblance to actual people, living or dead, or to businesses, companies, events, institutions, or locales is completely coincidental.

Kokomo, IN / Eric Hobbs — First Edition

ISBN 978-1794567214

Printed in the United States of America

*For Ray Bradbury,*
*who's horror was told with a wink and a smile.*

# 1.

Ms. Jackson was obese. Not fat, not overweight. Obese. Rob said she was so big she deserved her own zip code. AJ liked to call her Sags because folds of fat had begun to droop over her waistband. Even her face was swollen with the stuff, so big that her chin had all but disappeared. Making matters worse, she had bad skin. It was pocked with pimples and blackheads and scars left behind by battles with acne. And her hair? You could see through the stringy strands to her scaly, pink scalp. She was going bald like a middle-aged man.

I don't say these things to be mean. You may feel sorry for her now, but I promise you won't by the end. I only mention these things so you understand what Ms. Jackson was like before she moved away, before the network cooking show that made her a star. She was just a miserable lunch lady that everyone made fun of. Kids lobbed insults at her from the lunch line every day. We just happened to be the ones who finally pushed Ms. Jackson over the edge.

Looking back, I don't know how I ever became friends with Rob Barnett. One minute I was the new kid in school, the next I was hanging with some of the meanest kids I'd ever met. Not that it was all bad. When you're running with kids like Rob you don't get bullied nearly as much as everyone else. But you do have to sit back and watch. Sometimes that can be worse. Once, Rob caught Mike Tomlinson in the coat room, held him down, and shoved chewing gum into Mike's nose – gum he'd been chewing since the beginning of the day. I'll never forget the look in Mike's eyes. He begged me to help without saying a single word. Instead, I moved to the door to make sure no one was coming. Not my finest moment, I'll admit. But sadly, it wasn't my worst either.

Luckily most days weren't that bad. In fact, the day we finally pushed Ms. Jackson too far had unfolded with zero drama by the time lunch came around. I was the first to our table, digging around in my food when Rob plopped down beside me.

"Gabe says his mom didn't make him a meatball sub. Can you believe that? Stealing that sandwich is the only thing I have to look forward to on Monday. You don't think he's holding out on me, do you?"

I swallowed a mouthful of food. "I doubt he suddenly decided he's gonna keep it for himself."

"You're right," Rob said with a laugh. "He knows what would happen. What's Ms. Jackson cooking up today?"

Rob started picking through the food on my tray: meatloaf, cubed potatoes, this pile of lettuce with some shaved carrots that was supposed to pass for a salad. He popped a couple potatoes into his mouth without asking.

"Ugh! How can you eat this stuff?"

"Doesn't taste that bad to me."

Before I could say any more, Rob spit his food onto my tray then reached for my chocolate milk. Shaking my head in frustration, I covered my tray with a napkin. I was done eating whether I'd had enough or not.

After dusting off my milk, Rob shifted his attention to Ms. Jackson. Her back was to us as she worked to served up trays to sixth graders that were now filing into the cafeteria.

"Hey, Sags! When you gonna serve something that's actually worth eating? We know you didn't get that big eating this crap!"

Ms. Jackson kept her head down. She'd decided long ago she wasn't going to respond to comments like that. Instead, she

did her best to let them go in one ear and out the other.

Unfortunately for her, Rob wanted a reaction…

Rob snatched a couple more potatoes from my tray and began chucking them across the room.

The first one fell short of his target.

The second flew past her.

The third nailed Ms. Jackson in the head.

Some girls at a neighboring table rolled their eyes like they were disgusted with Rob's behavior. But after taking a quick moment to collect herself, Ms. Jackson just went about her business, continuing to serve up food to the kids in line – even those that were laughing at her.

Upset to see he would get no response, Rob pushed to his feet. "Whatever," he smirked. "I'm gonna see what Ben Savage's mom made him for lunch before he gets a chance to eat it himself. See you in English?"

I nodded a silent response then we bumped fists and Rob started away.

It bothered me to know he could get away with something like that. Ms. Jackson wasn't supposed to put up with Rob's antics the way she did. She wasn't a teacher, but she *was* an adult…

Ms. Jackson was supposed to teach bullies like Rob Barnett a lesson.

## 2.

Our English teacher took a much different approach when dealing with kids like Rob. If anyone dared insult Mr. Marsh he usually shot them down so fast they never thought to do it again. He was smart and funny and talked trash better than anyone. Probably one of the reasons why he was everyone's favorite.

"Take your seats, people. We've got a lot to cover today."

Mr. Marsh was leaning against his desk at the front of the room when the final bell rang. Rob waltzed through the door a few seconds after that.

"Nice of you to join us, Mr. Barnett."

"Yeah," Rob smirked. "I thought I'd grace you with my presence today."

"You don't get your grades up, you're going to be gracing us with your presence next year, too. I think I speak for all of your teachers when I say: please don't let that happen."

Everyone laughed as Rob started toward the empty desk beside mine. Personally, I wasn't paying much attention. A long, beat-up box of comic books at Mr. Marsh's feet had stolen my complete attention.

"Okay," Mr. Marsh began, "I know you guys are getting tired of the material we've been covering. My students always get this dead look in their eyes when we start reading Shakespeare. So… I figure it's time to mix it up with something new." He grabbed a stack of comics and began passing them out. "Some of the best stories being told today are unfolding in the pages of comic books. We're going to read them, familiarize ourselves with the structure of a comic story – then each of you will be responsible for publishing a comic of your own."

"What kind of comic?" someone asked. "Like a superhero book?"

"If you like. But remember: comics are a medium, not a genre. You can tell any kind of story you want. Adventure, fantasy, romance, horror."

He handed me a thin book titled *Tales from the Crypt*. The cover was tattered and creased, but the art was pretty dope: a funkified zombie reaching up from his grave to pull some helpless chick into the coffin beside him.

"We'll start with some quiet reading time today. But please, don't just blast through it. Spend as much time enjoying the art as you do reading the words. Art is the most important part of a comic. It's how the action unfolds."

Beside me, Rob was flipping through a copy of something called *Miracleman*. I was a little surprised to see him so interested. Usually he just sat there and scrolled through his phone.

"Hey Mr. Marsh?" Rob asked. "What's with these ads in the back?"

Mr. Marsh's mouth lifted into a nostalgic grin. "Those are old school. They used to be in the back of every comic. If you saw something you liked, you could cut out the offer and mail it in with your allowance."

Rob had his nose in the book again. "Yeah, but this stuff can't be real, right? I mean this one says it will give you the body of an Olympian in seven days. X-Ray glasses for a dollar. And what the heck is a Sea Monkey?"

Curious myself, I raised up in my seat so I could read over Rob's shoulder. Sure enough, his finger had landed on an illustration of these crazy looking creatures that lived in an underwater castle. The pink figures wore clothes like normal people, but they had long tails, webbed feet, and strange sprouts on top of their heads. *Instant Pets!* the ad promised. *Just add water!*

"Everyone ordered Sea Monkeys," Mr. Marsh explained.

"Did they look like that?" I asked.

"Of course not. Nothing you got lived up to the hype. But that was part of the fun. You always thought you were gonna stumble upon the one thing that actually worked."

Mr. Marsh moved to answer a girl who'd been waiting patiently with a question of her own. When he was gone, Rob looked over at me with a grin.

"What?"

I followed his pointing finger to find his attention had fallen on one of the most unbelievable offers in the comic: a machine called Dr. Drummond's Home Weight-Loss System. *Lose twenty pounds overnight – guaranteed!* The clunky machine looked like a medieval torture device. The main part of the machine featured a series of gears and pistons affixed to a hand crank. A coil of tubing extended from the machine, ending at an impossibly long needle.

"What's it do?" I asked. "Suck your fat?"

Looking about, Rob made sure no one was looking then slowly began to tear the ad from his comic.

"What are you doing?"

"You'll see."

21

"Man, these comics are super old. What If that's worth some money?"

But Rob didn't care.

He shoved the aged slip of paper into his pocket then slumped down in his seat like everything was normal. He couldn't hide his excitement, though. It was written in the mischievous grin that had darkened his face. Someone new was about to lose their lunch; or have chewing gum shoved up their nose…

Or worse.

# 3.

Rob told me to meet him behind the buses after school. When I got there, Jess and AJ were already waiting.

"Where's he at?" Jess asked impatiently. "I can't wait all day."

The rest of us walked to school, but Jess lived across town. If she spent too much time waiting on Rob, she'd have a two-hour hike in front of her.

"Here he comes," AJ said matter-of-factly.

Rob brushed by us and started into the teacher's parking lot. "C'mon."

The three of us hurried after him, ducking in and out of cars until we reached the ugliest bucket of rust I'd ever seen: Ms. Jackson's car.

"Dude," AJ began, "are you gonna tell us what's going on?"

Rob dug the weight-loss ad from his pocket and showed it to the others. Both giggled with excitement when they finally understood Rob's plan.

"Make sure no one's looking," Rob said.

Jess and AJ scanned the lot. The principal was talking with teachers near the school's entrance as kids poured out of the building. Parents had parked up and down the street, but they were all too busy looking for their kids to notice us.

After getting the go-ahead from Jess and AJ, Rob quickly pinned the ad to Ms. Jackson's cracked windshield. "Alright! Let's go! Go, go, go!"

We darted back the way we came, eventually taking cover behind one of the school buses still parked on the curb.

"I've only got a few more minutes," Jess reminded.

"It's okay," Rob said. "Ms. Jackson is always one of the first to leave."

A moment later, our lunch lady stepped out of the school.

Just watching her was enough to make my heart ache. Kids were racing out of the building all around her. In fact, they were moving so quickly Ms. Jackson appeared to be walking in slow motion. Her back was hunched; her steps short, nothing more than a shuffle across the concrete as she stepped into the parking lot.

One at a time, the bus engines roared to life nearby.

"I gotta go."

Jess started to leave, but Rob grabbed hold of her wrist. "Wait!"

By the time she reached her car, Ms. Jackson was out of breath. She actually had to stop, leaning on the back of her beat-up vehicle to rest.

AJ turned up his nose. "Has this woman never heard of a treadmill?"

We pulled a bit further into hiding, each of us interested to see how Ms. Jackson would react. Strangely, she stood up straight the moment her gaze landed on the pinned piece of paper. Color rushed into her pale cheeks.

"This is it!" Rob exclaimed.

Ms. Jackson removed the paper from her windshield. Her excitement disappeared the moment she started to read.

Rob and AJ erupted in laughter.

"She thought it was a love note," AJ cracked.

Seeing Rob was finally satisfied, Jess pulled from his grip. Unfortunately, she did this just as the buses started to move. She had to sprint after them if she was going to have a chance. "Wait!"

AJ smacked Rob's arm. "Look, look, look! She's keeping it!"

Sure enough, Ms. Jackson was pocketing the ad for Dr. Drummond's weight loss device.

"She thinks it's real!" Rob exclaimed. "She's gonna try and order one!"

AJ backed away, smiling. "Classic. Text me, okay?"

Rob and I nodded a response. Across the way, Ms. Jackson's car was belching dark smoke into the air as she pulled out of her spot.

"You think she saw us?" I asked.

"It's not like she's a teacher. She's the freakin lunch lady. What's she gonna do if she did?"

Rob tossed his bag over one shoulder and started down the walk. I moved in the opposite direction, ready to cross the parking lot when—

Ms. Jackson's car whipped around the corner, appearing from nowhere, tires screeching as it closed on me.

I froze, a deer in headlights, squeezing my eyes shut as if that would be enough to stop the car from splattering me across its hood.

When I was finally brave enough, I opened my eyes to discover luck was on my side. Ms. Jackson had hit the brakes just in time, her car stopping just inches before turning me into its permanent hood ornament.

I flashed a nervous smile, offering a half-hearted wave of thanks. But Ms. Jackson didn't respond. All she did was rage at me through the glass. It was like she'd only stopped to let me know it was her. Now she was ready to mash her chubby foot down on the gas and flatten me.

She didn't, of course. I quickly got out of her way, and Ms. Jackson turned the corner and pulled out of the lot for good. But there was something about that look through the glass that stayed with me. I spent the entire walk home checking over my shoulder to make sure she wasn't there. But she never was. And by the time I fell asleep that night I'd forgotten about the whole thing.

## 4.

It turns out Ms. Jackson spent the next several weeks devising a way to deal with us. "How are you boys doing today?"

We all looked up from our lunch to discover Ms. Jackson looming over us.

"Boys?" Jess smirked.

"I'm sorry," Ms. Jackson said. "You had your hoodie pulled so low I didn't know it was you. You shouldn't do that, you know? You're too pretty to be hiding behind anything."

Jess tossed back her hair, her expression softening. "Thanks."

"I'm only telling the truth. No need to thank me for that."

"What do you want?" Rob sneered.

Copying someone's homework, Rob had only glanced in the woman's direction. By then I think he'd forgotten all about the prank in the parking lot. He'd also missed the tray of desserts she'd brought from the kitchen: four pastries that looked like they belonged in one of those fancy restaurants. You know the kind? Where you have to dress up and your parents make you promise to be on your best behavior. The food stinks, but the desserts always make up for it.

"Well," Ms. Jackson continued, "I don't want to be a bother. It's just… well… I'm trying some new recipes, and I thought the four of you might try them and tell me what you think."

Rob continued with his homework, but the rest of us were raising up in our seats to get a good look at the goods. While the cakes were all different, each was topped with a creamy icing that was so fresh it was dripping down the sides.

"I'll give that chocolate cake a try," AJ said.

"Oh good!"

Ms. Jackson lowered the tray so each of us could take one of the desserts. I landed on something she called an apple crisp. To this day, I've never eaten anything that's tasted as good as that first dessert.

"Holy cow!" Jess exclaimed. "This is awesome!"

"You think so?" Ms. Jackson asked excitedly.

Mouths full, AJ and I answered with an emphatic nod.

"I was hoping you'd say that. Don't tell anyone, but I think I'm going to audition for one of those cooking shows you see on TV."

Jess talked between bites. "Really, Ms. Jackson? That would be cool, someone from town making it big like that. And if you keep cooking up stuff like this, you've totally got a chance."

"I'd like to bring you some more tomorrow. I've got plenty of recipes, and I'd love to get your opinions so I can perfect them before auditioning for the show."

This time AJ didn't wait to empty his mouth before answering. "Mhmm! I'll eat as many of these little beauties as you can cook up, Ms. Jackson."

Irritated to see that the lunch lady was still lingering about, Rob finally looked up from his work. "Is that why you finally decided to go on a diet? You know you've got to lose weight if you want to be on TV?"

The rest of us stared at him in disbelief. He was gonna ruin this for all of us. Ms. Jackson had lost a little weight, but Rob had not meant to compliment her.

"You can't just ask someone about their diet," Jess scolded.

"It's fine, Jessica. I've only been dieting a few weeks. It's nice to know someone has noticed."

Upset to see he hadn't hurt Ms. Jackson, Rob shook his head and went back to his math.

Meanwhile, Ms. Jackson spotted several kids who were waiting at the serving station to get their lunch. "Oh, looks like duty calls."

Already done with his cake, AJ was now scooping icing off his plate with one of his fingers so he could get every drop of the sugary goodness. "You really should try one of these."

"I will," Rob said.

AJ dropped his plate to the table. "If you don't eat yours, I'm going to."

"Okay! Fine!"

Rob cut a piece of his lemon tart and shoveled it into his mouth.

"There! Are you…"

His words trailed off as he got his first taste. When Jess and AJ saw the stunned look on his face, they began to laugh.

"See what we mean," I said.

"There's no way Ms. Jackson made this!"

Rob scooped another bite into his mouth. Then another. He was already halfway through the dish and had forgotten all about his math.

"The icing!" he exclaimed. "Holy mother of jeez!"

The rest of us laughed, amused to see Rob so taken aback. When I looked over to see if Ms. Jackson was still paying attention I saw that she was too focused on her work again to see Rob had finally given in.

But she was smiling. Looking back, I realize that was the first time I'd ever seen a smile on Ms. Jackson's face.

Unfortunately, it wouldn't be the last.

# 5.

If Ms. Jackson thought she could bribe a bunch of eighth-grade bullies with sugar, if she thought we'd be nice to her as long as she served our sweet tooth…

She was right.

For weeks, the lunch lady gifted us with a new tray of treasures each day. And for weeks, we scarfed them down with delight.

Not once did we think to ask: can you have too much of a good thing?

I don't know how the others felt, but I started to notice some warning signs that we might be overdoing it.

Ms. Jackson's sweets always left me feeling energized, like I was strong enough to take on the world. Unfortunately, that rarely lasted. After a while I would become sluggish and tired. By the time school was out, all I wanted to do was get home so I could fall onto the couch and sleep for hours on end.

A few weeks after our first tray, I started to notice some other changes too. Rob wasn't one for gym class, but AJ and I lived for those Friday afternoons. We were both two of the fastest, most athletic kids in school. We loved to compete. Some of my favorite childhood memories occurred in that gymnasium, but most of those memories came before Ms. Jackson and her delicious desserts.

It happened over time, but eventually AJ and I weren't as fast as we used to be. All at once, kids we had dominated all year were able to keep up with us. I'll never forget the day we lost our first game of football chase. It was like we were running in quicksand. The more we pushed, the slower we ran. When it was over we had to watch Jay Archer and Randall Price celebrate like they'd just been crowned champions of the world.

Then we threw up in the locker room.

As good as Ms. Jackson's treats could be, they didn't taste nearly as good on the way up as they did on the way down.

But Rob was the first to show signs that something might be seriously wrong.

At the time, it felt simple enough. After all, we were thirteen. We were going to get breakouts every once in a while. But this was different. About a month after we'd become Ms. Jackson's personal taste testers, Rob came to school sporting one of the biggest pimples I'd ever seen. In fact, it wasn't one pimple at all. A group of them had joined forces, all sprouting up in one spot to create a puss-oozing mass on the side of his face.

In a twisted bit of bad luck, Rob's breakout bloomed on the day he was to present his comic to the rest of the class. Truthfully, his comic was pretty cool. He'd created a superhero named Night Eyes. An abused teenager who'd run away from home, Rob's creation saved children who weren't able to escape abuse on their own. I could tell Mr. Marsh was impressed, but no one else noticed. All they could do was stare in disbelief at Rob's giant zit.

When he was done presenting, Rob hurried back to his seat and slumped down behind his desk.

"Very nice!" Mr. Marsh said excitedly. "Does anyone have any questions?"

A few hands shot up.

"Yes. Sean?"

Sean Parker turned in his seat. "Umm… what does Night Eyes do when he saves the kids? He breaks them out of these abusive homes, right? Does that mean they end up homeless like him?"

Rob shook his head. "No, he finds them a place to stay. That's what's so sad about the whole thing. He's giving these kids a second chance, but he's just… I don't know… he's too scared to take that chance himself."

This seemed to move Mr. Marsh even more. "That's awesome, Rob. Great work. Truly. You may pass my class yet."

Rob laughed.

"You know: there's no reason you have to stop just because the assignment is finished. If you enjoy writing stories like this you should keep going. I'd be excited to see what comes next."

Rob nodded a silent reply as Mr. Marsh pointed to a girl who'd been patiently waiting to ask another question. "Jennifer. Go."

"What happened to your face?"

"Yeah," Gabe added. "You should get that looked at."

Rob scowled at Gabe from across the room. "I'm gonna give you something that needs looked at if you don't shut up."

Laughing, Gabe mocked surrender with his hands in the air. I couldn't believe it. Normally Gabe tried to avoid Rob at all costs. If he saw Rob coming down the hall, Gabe turned to walk the other way. Now he was antagonizing Rob. And other kids were ready to do the same…

"That doesn't even look like a zit," someone said.

"It's like a boil," a squeaky voice added.

"A boil ready to burst."

Rob's jaw clenched.

"That's enough," the teacher said sternly.

Danny Jacobs raised his hand from the seat beside Rob. "Mr. Marsh," he began, "can I move seats?"

"Why?"

"I don't want to be this close if that thing bursts. It looks like something out of a horror movie. What if it's contagious?"

Rob covered the distance between them in a flash. He lunged at Danny, yanking the boy from his seat with such force that his desk tipped onto its side. His fist was ready to fly when Mr. Marsh finally stepped in. The teacher pulled the boys apart then twisted Rob's arm behind his back and pinned him to the wall.

"What are you doing?" Rob screamed. "I didn't do anything!"

"Are you kidding me?" Mr. Marsh asked.

Looking stunned, Danny slowly backed away from them.

Rob struggled to break free, but he was no match for our teacher. Mr. Marsh was sure to keep a firm grip on Rob's arm as he began marching him toward the door. "Amy, you're in charge. If anyone leaves their seat, I want to know about it."

Rob passed his eyes across the class on his way out of the room. I couldn't tell if he was angry or sad. A little of both, I guess. Not because he was being sent to the principal's office. Rob had more write-ups than anyone in the school's history. No, Rob Barnett had finally gotten a brief taste of what it was like to be on the other side of things, and he didn't like it… not one bit.

## 6.

If Rob thought he'd be alone with his problems, he could have taken comfort in the fact that the rest of his friends would be joining him soon. Within a few days, everyone at our lunch table had developed ugly breakouts of their own.

And our transformations didn't stop there.

Usually one of our school's biggest trendsetters, Jess started coming to school in baggy sweatpants. She wouldn't say why, but I suspected it was because her skinny jeans no longer fit. In truth, we'd all put on a lot of weight.

And we weren't the only ones going through changes.

"Ms. Jackson looks so good," I said.

The lunch lady had just delivered another tray of desserts to our table and was now hurrying back to her serving station. Hurrying, something she could only dream of doing before.

"She's on a diet," Jess said. "Remember?"

"I know, but… does that seem normal to you? I bet she's lost like a hundred pounds in the last three months. That doesn't make sense."

AJ wasn't so sure. "It only looks like she's lost that much because she's dressing like a lady for the first time in her life."

47

Ms. Jackson *had* made some pretty drastic changes to her wardrobe as well. She'd traded those loose t-shirts for form-fitting blouses; her slacks for nice skirts; her white hospital shoes for high heels. She was working hard to land her own cooking show and was already dressing the part.

"It's not just that," Jess said. "Even her skin looks good."

A nearby table of seventh-grade boys had turned to watch Ms. Jackson cross the room. Each wore a mischievous grin like they were getting away with something. A lot of boys had started showing an interest in Ms. Jackson. No one would call her skinny. Not yet. But she was attractive. The woman who had disgusted kids just months ago now had a fan club, dozens of boys with a crush.

Rob was halfway through his lemon crème pie when he finally decided to chime in. "I hear she's dating the shop teacher, Mr. Meadows."

"That's just a rumor," I said. "We asked him in third period."

"Then why was she spending so much time in his class?"

"Mr. Meadows says she just wanted help with some sort of project she's putting together."

"Yeah right," Rob smirked.

"You guys know this is her last year, right?" Jess asked.

Our heads snapped up.

"What?!"

"I heard she's moving. Maybe she really got on one of those shows."

The rest of us shared a sad look. We didn't have to say a word to know we were all thinking the exact same thing: no more desserts.

"Think she'll give her recipes to the woman who replaces her?" I asked.

Sneering, Rob shook his head. "What do you think, genius? Those recipes are her ticket out of here. You really think she's gonna share?"

"Maybe that's okay," Jess said. "Am I the only one who doesn't think her stuff is as good as it used to be?"

Rob gestured to her clean plate. "You could have fooled us, Jess."

Shame washed over her. "I keep telling myself I won't have any more, but on Sunday night Ms. Jackson's desserts are the only thing I can think about."

"If you stop eating her stuff, that just means there's more for us."

Rob slapped AJ five. "Right!"

Jess looked down at her lap. "It's not worth it. I look like a mutant. I feel terrible all the time. Half the time I eat so much that I throw up between classes. Plus, I don't know if you've noticed, but I've gained a bunch of weight."

Rob shook his head. "Everyone noticed. You started wearing your dad's shirts to school just to hide that roll that flops over your shorts."

"You aren't looking too great yourself, Rob!"

Back at her work station, Ms. Jackson was laughing with some boys in her line. You might even say she was flirting with them. Whatever it was, one thing was certain: she had them eating out of the palm of her hand.

Rob pushed to his feet. "Whatever," he said. "I guarantee Ms. Jackson is getting high on her own supply. She's never looked better. All we have to do is figure out what she's doing, and we'll be good."

"How are we gonna do that?" I asked.

"Don't worry," Rob explained. "I'll figure something out."

# 7.

On the last day of school, Rob and I went looking for Ms. Jackson.

The halls were littered with trash, graded papers and tattered folders kids had pulled from their lockers and tossed to the floor. The Last Day Paper Fight was a tradition in our school. Normally, Rob and I would have been in the thick of the battle. But this year we had far more pressing concerns.

"You think she's still here?"

"Yeah," Rob replied. "She never leaves until the final bell rings."

We slinked through the door and into the kitchen.

"Hello? Ms. Jackson?"

The sterile room was empty, everything put away for summer. Rules said we weren't supposed to be there, and my intuition was screaming the same. Something about the sharp knives and the walk-in freezer waiting to trap us filled me with a sense of dread. Silly, I know, but the silence was deafening. Then—

We rounded the corner to find Ms. Jackson blocking our path.

Startled, both of us jumped.

"Holy heck!" Rob exclaimed.

It took me a moment to recover. When I finally did, I saw the lunch lady had a butcher knife gripped tightly in her right hand.

"Sorry," she said. "I didn't mean to scare you."

"Didn't you hear us calling?" Rob asked.

Ms. Jackson shook her head, but that answer made me even more uncomfortable than the knife. Of course she'd heard us. You could hear a pin drop in that kitchen.

"I'm surprised you boys have stuck around," she said. "Aren't you ready for summer?"

"We were hoping you could help us with something first," Rob explained.

"You're here for one last dessert, aren't you?"

"Not exactly. We… well… you're looking so great, Ms. Jackson."

"That's very kind."

"I don't know… you looked so different at the start of the year… you've got to tell us your secret."

Carefully touching the tip of her knife with one finger, she began to twirl it between both hands. "Oh, I couldn't do that Robert."

"Why not?"

"Can you imagine what would happen if I shared my diet drinks with you?"

"So it's a drink?" Rob asked.

Ms. Jackson covered her mouth. "See? I've already given too much away."

"You don't have to give it to us. Just tell us what it's called."

"I'm sorry, Robert. I can't do that either. It wouldn't be right. Why don't you sit down with your mother and see if she can—"

Before she could finish, Rob blew up in anger and kicked the freezer door. "Because my mother didn't lose a hundred pounds since Christmas! Because the only reason we look like this is because of your stupid desserts. You owe us!"

For a brief moment Ms. Jackson looked like she was about to plunge her knife into Rob's neck. But the darkness was gone as quickly as it appeared. She took a deep breath. "Are you sure there isn't something else I can help you with?"

"Why else would we be talking to you on the last day of school?"

A dark grin split the woman's face. "Why else, indeed."

# 8.

I knew Rob wasn't going to let this go, but even I was surprised when I learned how far he was willing to go.

"You mind telling me what's so important you had to pull me away from my deathmatch?" AJ asked. "I was killing everyone."

"We're going to break into Ms. Jackson's house," Rob said matter-of-factly.

Jess couldn't believe it. "What? No! No way! I'm not doing that."

"Fine. But when we find her diet stuff and her face cream and whatever else she's using, don't come begging to us. We aren't gonna share crap."

Jess looked to AJ for some sort of support.

"I'm supposed to play JV football in the fall. I can't show up out of shape."

"Do you know how vicious high school girls are to freshmen?" Rob asked Jess. "You show up with bad skin and greasy hair and they'll eat you alive. You need Ms. Jackson's help more than anyone."

While hesitant, Jess eventually gave in with a nod. After that, we were off.

A full moon rose into the sky as we walked across town. Big and orange, the bright disk slipped in and out of the clouds to light our way.

Most of the homes in Ms. Jackson's neighborhood were in bad shape with junk strewn across their yards. Others were abandoned, their yards just a patch of overgrowth, their windows boarded so no one could get inside.

We passed several strangers along the way. One guy smelled like gym shorts and asked if we were lost. Another was pulling a mountain of plastic bags in a little red wagon. Strangely, all he did was stare at us from beneath a flickering streetlight. Yeah, it was just as creepy as it sounds.

Eventually Rob stopped us just outside a little house on a shadowy cul-de-sac. Its paint was peeling. Shingles were missing from its roof. Its rusted screen door was hanging askew.

"This is it," Rob said.

"How do you know?" I asked.

"The internet?"

Rob's tone dared me to press him any further than that.

Jess pointed to one of the windows. The lights were on inside. If this really was her house, Ms. Jackson appeared to be home.

"How are we supposed to break in if she's here?" Jess asked.

"We'll wait for her to leave."

"And if she doesn't?"

"Then we'll wait 'til she goes to sleep."

My stomach sank. This was way beyond stealing lunches and copying homework. If we got caught we were going to end up in the back of a police car. I was desperate to get out of there, searching my mind for any excuse to head home. But when Rob found a place to hide I joined him with everyone else. As if it wasn't bad enough I never stopped him. Now I wasn't even strong enough to walk away.

The four of us hid in the shadow of a neighbor's fence, watching from across the street until—

"Hey!" Jess whispered. "Look!"

The garage door on Ms. Jackson's house had begun to rise.

"Get down!" Rob ordered.

We pulled together in the darkness.

When the door was finally open, Ms. Jackson backed her car down the drive and started up the street. A moment later, she disappeared around the corner.

"Time to make our move," Rob said.

The four of us pushed to our feet and hurried that way.

"Why'd she leave the garage open?" I asked.

"Are you kidding? Who cares? That's our way in!"

Rob led us into the garage and quickly pushed through the door into Ms. Jackson's house. AJ and Jess slipped into the darkness behind him, but I stopped short of the doorway.

Something wasn't right, and it wasn't my conscious this time.

This all seemed a bit too easy.

"Hurry up!" Rob said. "Before someone sees!"

Stepping through the door, the smell hit me like a ton of bricks. Something sweet lingered just beneath the surface, but the house was dominated by the pungent scent of rotten meat.

"Jeez!" AJ exclaimed. "What is that?"

"I don't know," Rob said.

"It's making my eyes water."

The cloudy window allowed a sliver of pale moonlight into the living room. The walls were bare, nothing but a few hooks where pictures had been. Sealed moving boxes were scattered and stacked in columns throughout the room.

"You two check her bedroom."

Jess and AJ quickly obeyed as Rob and I hurried down the hall into the tiny bathroom. He immediately pulled open drawers, dumping their contents onto the tile floor.

"What are you doing?"

"Check the medicine cabinet," Rob said without answering.

I pulled open the mirror then carefully sifted through Ms. Jackson's night creams and perfumes. Rob continued making a mess on the floor.

"There's nothing here," I said.

"Really?"

"There's some wrinkle cream but nothing for acne."

"All I've got are a bunch of hair ties and make-up," Rob said.

I was about to says something when Jess appeared in the doorway.

*"Dude! She's back!"*

Rob sprang to his feet. Together we booked down the hall just in time to see headlights hit the living room window, flooding the house with light as Ms. Jackson turned into the driveway. AJ led us toward the front door but came to an abrupt halt when he saw Ms. Jackson had parked in the driveway. She'd be climbing out of her car just in time to see us stumbling out of her house.

Back door!" I yelled. "C'mon!"

We rushed into the next room. Apparently, Ms. Jackson had only begun packing the kitchen. Not that I noticed. That horrific smell was only intensifying as we got deeper into the house. Then my gaze fell on the boiling pot on her stove.

The others wheeled about in terror when they heard the clip-clop of Ms. Jackson's heels on the sidewalk, the jingle of her house keys.

*"We gotta hide, man! We gotta hide!"*

Jess and AJ ducked for cover. Rob bolted for the pantry. But I couldn't move. That pot on the stove had become my sole worry in life.

"Brody! What are you doing?"

Ignoring AJ, I inched toward the stove with a growing sense of dread. Whatever

Ms. Jackson was cooking in that pot: it wasn't food. Bloated streamers of fat were swimming in grey liquid that was just about to bubble over.

"Brody... look..."

It was the worry in Rob's voice that finally pulled me away from the unholy concoction in that pot. He'd opened the pantry door, intent on hiding inside. But he'd quickly discovered he wanted no part of that tiny closet...

A wobbly chair stood in the center of Ms. Jackson's pantry. Three industrial-sized buckets were placed nearby, the type you might see on a construction site.

And then, there was the device.

"Now you know my secret ingredient."

Rob and I spun around to find Ms. Jackson standing in the doorway. Somehow she looked even better than she had that afternoon. Oddly, she didn't seem too concerned that the four of us had broken into her home.

"Is that… is that what I think it is?" Rob asked.

Chuckling, Ms. Jackson moved into the pantry. AJ and Jess rose to their feet. There was no reason to hide now.

"What is it?" Jess asked.

"Yeah," AJ added. "What's going on?"

Ms. Jackson struggled to lift the device. It was made of metal and much larger than the picture in that comic book had led us to believe. But other than that, Dr. Drummond's Home Weight-Loss System was exactly as advertised.

She dropped the heavy machine onto her kitchen counter. "I supposed I owe you children a thank you. I never would have tried something so drastic if it weren't for the four of you."

AJ looked like he was about to jump out of his shoes. "Will someone please tell me what's going on? W-what's in those buckets?"

Ms. Jackson smiled. "The same thing that's cooking up on my stove."

Just then the oven timer chimed.

"Oh," Ms. Jackson said excitedly. "It looks like you got here just in time."

Grabbing an oven mitt from a nearby drawer, Ms. Jackson opened the oven to reveal a tray of four desserts waiting inside. She carefully removed them, setting the tray down on her counter. Then Ms. Jackson took a bag of sugar from her cabinet and slowly began to pour it into the pot on the stove.

I looked about the kitchen as Ms. Jackson began to stir. Everything was right there in front of me. The reason for Ms. Jackson's stunning transformation. The explanation for our own troubles. I watched in horror as she began to smear cream from the pot onto each of the waiting desserts. Somehow sugar had been enough to turn that horrific concoction into the icing…

The same icing we'd spent the last several months devouring.

Only it wasn't icing.

It was Ms. Jackson's fat.

"A little sugar always helps the medicine go down, don't you think?"

I lunged for the sink, barely making it before my dinner came up in a wave. When I was done, I turned to face the others.

"Wait," AJ stuttered. "It's… that's…. no… no!"

"Why would you do this to us?" Jess asked.

"Oh Jessica, are you really that upset?"

Ms. Jackson continued to paint her sweetened insides onto the pastries she'd pulled from the oven. Somehow, the rancid smell that had greeted us was now gone. All that remained was the scrumptious smell of her goodies.

And my mouth…

I couldn't believe it.

I'd just puked up my guts, but my mouth was already starting to water.

Ms. Jackson set the tray of desserts on a nearby table. "Why don't you kids pull up a chair and dig in one last time."

I furrowed my brow. Was she serious or just insane?

Either way, Jess and AJ seemed to be considering it.

"You're nuts!" Rob shouted. "We're not eating that stuff!"

"But that's why you're here…"

"We came because you said you were hiding diet drinks!"

"Nonsense." Ms. Jackson stepped close enough to whisper in Rob's ear. "We both know what you're *really* after."

Rob shook his head. "No… no way… I'm not doing it."

But even I could tell he was starting to weaken.

"I think you will," Ms. Jackson explained. "And when I'm gone and you've moved on to the big school across town, you'll find something just as bad. Maybe something worse. It doesn't matter that you know it's bad. You'll just keep eating. From now on you four will be just as ugly on the outside as you are within."

Rob wanted to say something more, but the words seemed to catch in his throat. When he didn't respond, Ms. Jackson moved her mischievous gaze to Jess and AJ. Both of my friends had moved closer to the table.

"Go on," Ms. Jackson prodded. "I made them for you."

Both descended on the tray, each snatching up a dessert and shoving it into their mouth. Satisfied, Ms. Jackson shifted her attention to Rob once more.

"You came all this way. Are you really going to leave empty-handed?"

Rob turned toward me. His anger and defiance had completely melted away. He looked helpless, just like Mike in the coat room. Just like Gabe in the cafeteria. Just like Ms. Jackson before she'd decided to exact her sweet revenge.

"Don't do it," I said.

Without a word, Rob stepped toward the table of desserts.

The others were scarfing desserts so fast that their faces were now covered in icing, covered in Ms. Jackson's secret ingredient. Rob grabbed a piece of cake and chomped down on it like he was a predator attacking its prey.

"Rob!" I shouted. "You know what's in that? What are you doing?"

My friends acted like they didn't hear me at all. Their eyes had glazed over. All they did was smack their lips and stuff their faces.

Beaming, Ms. Jackson took a spot beside me. "Don't judge them, dear."

"I'm going to tell people what you did to us."

"Is that really what you're worried about? Or are you concerned one of your friends might get greedy and eat the cake I baked just for you?"

I fought so hard to hold onto my anger, but it was slipping away like a memory that disappears into the darkness of your mind. All I could think about was how good those desserts smelled. How good they looked. How good I knew they had to taste.

The lunch lady leaned into me so I could feel her breath on the back of my neck. "What's the danger in eating one more?"

A single tear streamed down my cheek. "I'll just have a bite."

The lunch lady smiled. "Whatever you think is best."

Tears streaming, I stepped forward and took a seat beside my friends. They'd been good enough to leave the remaining dessert alone. And while I did believe I would only take one bite, I'm ashamed to say that's not what happened. As soon as that sweet icing hit my tongue, I knew one bite would never be enough. I knew my friends and I wouldn't leave Ms. Jackson's house until we'd licked the bowl clean.

## FIN

# Hungry for more scares?

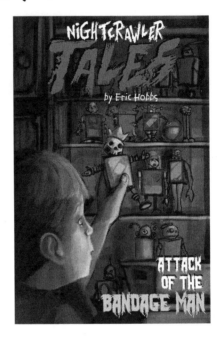

A boring shopping trip leads to a fascinating discovery when Ben finds a one-of-a-kind toy hiding in an antique shop his mother frequents. An avid collector, Ben brings the toy home, only to learn he's put his family in danger when the morbid toy goes through a horrific transformation once the sun's gone down.

This action-packed creep-fest is the perfect follow up to *Lunchroom Revenge*. Grab it today!

Look for more *Tales* soon. Collect them all!

# HORROR ON THE GROM!

Did you like this book enough to tell your friends about it? Share a picture with *88 Keys* on Instagram. Be sure to tag us and we'll share your pic with our followers too. We've got a stash of cool prizes for the best snaps, so be creative! The scarier, the better. Just please, for the love of everything holy...

### *...NO MORE DUCK FACES!*

**instagram.com/nightcrawlertales**
**facebook.com/erichobbs**

# ALSO BY ERIC HOBBS

# ABOUT THE AUTHOR

Eric Hobbs is an American author of horror stories for children. Nothing excites him more than an angry letter from parents who think his work is too scary for their kids.

Made in the USA
Monee, IL
25 June 2020